Waiting for Carver Boyd

Books by Thomas Hauser

About Boxing

The Black Lights: Inside the World of
Professional Boxing

Muhammad Ali: His Life and Times

Muhammad Ali: Memories

Muhammad Ali: In Perspective

Muhammad Ali & Company

A Beautiful Sickness

A Year At The Fights

Brutal Artistry

The View From Ringside

Chaos, Corruption, Courage, and Glory

The Lost Legacy of Muhammad Ali

I Don't Believe It, But It's True

The Vikki LaMotta Story (with Vikki LaMotta)

The Greatest Sport of All

The Boxing Scene

An Unforgiving Sport

General Non-Fiction

Missing

The Trial of Patrolman Thomas Shea

For Our Children (with Frank Macchiarola)

The Family Legal Companion

Final Warning: The Legacy of Chernobyl
(with Dr Robert Gale)

Arnold Palmer: A Personal Journey

Confronting America's Moral Crisis
(with Frank Macchiarola)

Healing: A Journal of Tolerance and Understanding

Miscellaneous

With This Ring (with Frank Macchiarola)

A God To Hope For

Fiction

Ashworth & Palmer

Agatha's Friends

The Beethoven Conspiracy

THOMAS HAUSER

Waiting for
Carver Boyd

BOOKS

This is a work of fiction. Other than the occasional use of actual names and places, the incidents and other characters portrayed in this book are wholly fictional.

First published in Great Britain in 2010 by
JR Books, 10 Greenland Street, London NW1 0ND

Copyright © 2010 Thomas Hauser

Thomas Hauser has asserted his moral right to be identified as the Author of this Work in accordance with the Copyright Designs and Patents Act 1988.

A catalogue record for this book is available from the British Library.

ISBN 978-1-906779-81-8

1 3 5 7 9 10 8 6 4 2

Printed in Great Britain by Clays Ltd, St Ives plc

I've had some wonderful teachers
on my journey through the sweet science;
men and women who have opened their hearts to me
and taught me what they know about boxing.

This book is dedicated to all of them with thanks.

Waiting for Carver Boyd

They said there would never be another Mike Tyson. They were wrong. Carver Boyd was the first great heavyweight of the new millennium. In the ring, he was as good as Tyson ever was. Outside the ring, he was worse. I fought him. This is my story.

Part One

My life changed on a Thursday night in Jersey City, although I didn't know it at the time.

I was twenty-one years old and fighting in a hotel ballroom that had been converted into a boxing arena for the night. There were six fights on the card. I was in the main event. Local prospect, undefeated; six feet three inches tall, 205 pounds. I'd just crossed the line that separates cruiserweights from heavyweights. Probably, in a few years, I'd weigh 220.

I was fighting a guy named Horace Gibbs; a big scary-looking ex-con from Cleveland with nine wins in twelve fights. His muscles had muscles. A casual observer with compassion would have feared for my safety. Except the line on Gibbs was that he wasn't very good. Menacing stare, weak chin, not much of a puncher. I staggered him with a righthand in round one and knocked him down twice in round two. After the second knockdown, his corner threw in the towel.

Four days later, I drove over to Englewood Cliffs to do some errands. It was a sunny spring day, a little after noon. I didn't have to be at the gym until three o'clock. So I decided to buy a sandwich and eat it in one of the vest-pocket parks overlooking the Hudson River.

I stopped in a deli, bought lunch, and went back outside. That's when I saw a woman about my age on the sidewalk walking toward me.

She saw me the same moment that I saw her.

She was as beautiful as any woman who ever walked on the face of the earth.

Tall with long auburn hair and a body that I won't try to describe because words wouldn't do it justice.

Her face was as dreamlike as the rest of her.

The distance between us narrowed and there was a flash of recognition in her eyes.

"You're the fighter," she said.

I'm a fighter. Life has come at me hard at times. I have certain God-given physical gifts and I've worked to develop my craft.

I was born in Newark, not exactly the garden spot of the world. I have no idea who my father was. I'm not sure my mother knew either. She was a single parent; Italian-American with some Irish and Polish thrown in. After I was born, she moved in with a fifty-something woman named Catherine Cerabone. Catherine took care of me during the day while my mother was at work. Then my mother would come home and Catherine went out to a 6:00pm-to-midnight shift as a cleaning woman in a local office building.

One day when I was four years old, my mother didn't come home. Two policemen came to the apartment instead. Some neighbors arrived. Everyone seemed upset. I remember being scared. And I remember thinking that everything would be all right in the end because Catherine was there.

Everything wasn't all right. My mother had been killed crossing the street when a drunk driver ran a red light. I was her only known relative. She left no will. The social workers decided that my best interests would be served if I was placed in foster care with Catherine.

For the next few years, whenever I was somewhere that I'd gone to with my mother, I'd look for her. After I started pre-school, each day when I walked out of the building, I'd scan the faces of mothers waiting for their children to see if I could find her. Eventually, the only image I had of her in my mind came from a photograph of the two of us together. The photo was in my bedroom in a frame on top of my bureau. One day, when I was eleven, I put the photo in the bottom drawer. It made me sad to look at it.

When I was eight years old, Catherine enrolled me in a program called Project Pride that was the creation of a sportswriter named Jerry Izenberg. Izenberg had written for the *Newark Star-Ledger* since the early 1960s and wanted to give something back to the community he'd grown up in. Project Pride was his baby. It consisted of after-school activities two afternoons each week in schools throughout the city. The sessions covered everything from reading and math to life lessons in cooking and hygiene.

The kids in Project Pride were mostly black with a few whites and Latinos thrown in. A week after I joined the program, "Mr. Izenberg" came to visit and I was introduced to him as a new member.

I was in one of my wise-ass moods.

"Does anyone call you Izzy?" I queried.

"No! Does anyone call you banana-brain?" he countered.

I started to laugh.

"What's so funny?" he demanded.

"You."

"Is that good or bad?"

"It's good," I told him. "I like you."

"I like you too. Make sure you keep it that way."

Basically, I was a good kid but a contradiction of sorts. I was a natural athlete, but not particularly interested in team sports. I had exemplary grades in school, but also got into fights. Not a lot of fights, I told myself. Two or three a year. I saw myself as a protector and someone who stood up for what was right. The social worker who had my foster-care file said that there was a lot of anger in me and once asked me where it came from.

Send me back in a time-travel bubble and I could answer that question today. Let's see. I never knew my father. My mother died when I was four. I'm being raised poor in Newark, New Jersey, by a woman old enough to be my grandmother. Anger? You figure it out.

Back then, I just shrugged.

I was fourteen when I started high school. Ninth grade was different from what had come before. The older kids were more menacing and tougher. Johnny Bruton was sixteen years old with the musculature of a grown man and skin the color of bitter chocolate. He'd been in and out of reform school for a variety of reasons. It figured that, once he came of age, he'd wind up in the big house.

One afternoon when school was letting out, I saw Bruton hassling a girl on the sidewalk. She started to walk away. He followed and patted her on the ass. She slapped him. He slapped her back.

"Why don't you leave her alone," I said.

Bruton turned and walked toward me. "Did I ask for your opinion?"

"I don't think you should hit a girl."

He smiled. "Anything you say."

In the distance, a police siren was wailing. Someone had called 911.

Bruton turned as if to walk away. Then he swiveled

and sucker-punched me flush on the nose. Bone cracked. Blood started spurting.

I charged him and he threw me to the ground.

The cops arrived and sorted things out. Bruton was arrested. I wasn't, but my physical pain and humiliation were complete.

Several days later, Jerry Izenberg saw me with tape holding my realigned nosebone in place.

"What happened?" he asked.

"I want to learn how to fight."

"Maybe you should learn how to fight less."

"No; I want to learn how to box."

I explained to Jerry what had happened. He talked with my social worker and Catherine Cerabone. On a cold December day after my nose had healed, he brought me to a small gym in Newark. The sidewalk outside was littered with paper and broken glass. Inside, there was a boxing ring and some equipment. A shower and toilet stall were at the far end of the room adjacent to thirty-or-so metal lockers. There were four benches and some folding chairs. The smell of disinfectant and body odor filled the air.

A tall slender black man about forty years old was standing by the ring. Jerry introduced him to me as

Turner Gates. "I'll leave the two of you alone to talk and be back in an hour," he said.

Gates gestured for me to sit beside him on one of the benches. He had a kind face.

"So . . . Jerry tells me that you want to be a fighter."

"Yes, sir."

"Why?"

"I want to be able to beat people up."

"Do you want to beat me up?"

"No."

"Who do you want to beat up?"

"Anyone who hits me."

"What if the person who hits you has a gun or a knife?"

I didn't answer.

"That's something to think about. You know, I was a bad kid who did some things I shouldn't have done. And then I got in big trouble before I was saved like people are trying to save you now."

"I'm not a bad kid."

"No. But you might become one. Jerry tells me that . . ."

There followed a list of my transgressions, including a few that I didn't know Jerry was aware of.

"What we want to do," Gates continued, "is channel all of the emotion that goes into your anger in a more constructive way. So let me tell you a few things about boxing and how we do things here."

"Boxing isn't just a sport. It's a lifestyle for anyone who does it right. Don't look for an easy way to do things, because there's no easy way to be a fighter. You've got to train right. You've got to live right. It's about sacrifice. If you come to the gym every day after school, five days a week, I'll be here for you. If you can't come, you call. Tell me you're not coming and why. I'm not going to train you to be a fighter. I'm going to teach you. If you show me respect, I'll show you respect. If you don't show me respect, you're gone."

"You treat this gym like it's your home. You don't throw paper or anything else on the floor. If you see something on the floor, you bend over, pick it up, and throw it in the trash. If you fight outside the gym, you can't fight in it. Anybody who steals anything in my gym or anywhere else; I report them to the police. You get no chances to fuck up. Is that clear?"

"Yes, sir."

Turner Gates smiled and extended his hand. "You can call me Turner. Everyone else does. Any questions?"

"What did you do that was bad?"

"Someday, when you're older, maybe I'll tell you about it."

"Were you ever in jail?"

"No. But I should have been."

So five days a week, every week, I went to the gym after school. I thought Turner would start by teaching me how to jab. I was wrong. The first few weeks were about balance, distance, and movement. This is how you stand; this is the way to hold your hands; this is how you move forward; this is how you move backward. No punches.

Then he taught me how to jab.

"Boxing isn't about hitting people," he counselled. "It's about hurting people when you hit them. Don't flick your jab. A good jab is like smashing someone in the face with a two-by-four."

Each day, there was more.

"Always remember; the best thing in boxing is to not get hit. But I've been watching fights for a long time and every fighter I've ever seen got hit. You might be the first one not to, but I doubt it. So get used to it and throw back . . . You don't need skill to work hard. But working hard will help you develop your skills . . . Once the bell rings, you show no mercy, no compassion. You can't have a conscience in the ring."

After four months, Turner told me that I was ready to spar. The guy in the opposite corner was a journeyman fighter who occasionally worked out in the gym; a professional named Frankie Harris. Later, I realized it had been safer for me that way. Frankie was babysitting. An amateur might not have been as gentle.

The months passed. The sparring got harder. Guys my age and older threw punches at me, and I fired back.

Nothing in life prepares you for getting smacked in the face except getting smacked in the face. And it hurts more when the guy doing the smacking has been trained in the art of throwing punches. Turner was teaching me to act unnaturally; to rid myself of certain instincts and assimilate new ones. I had to counter the urge to bail out when someone was throwing punches at me and, at times, draw closer when I was being hurt to cut down on my opponent's leverage. Every punch I threw had to be followed instantaneously by a

13

defensive maneuver. When I got hit hard, I had to pretend like I didn't feel it. Or if I felt it, that it didn't matter.

"Do you give in to the pain, or do you fight it?" Turner asked rhetorically. "If you give in to pain, you can't be a fighter."

Ten months after I started in the gym, I had my first amateur fight. I won it, and then I won some more. I was fast with pretty good power. I could take a punch. And Turner was putting a solid foundation under me. "I like what I see," he told me after one of my wins. "You've got some fighter in you."

I lost three amateur fights. The first "L" on my record came in year one when I was outslicked by a more experienced boxer, who was a southpaw to boot. A year after that, when I was sixteen, I got stopped. I wasn't happy about it. I went down from a big righthand, got up, and the referee waved it off. Maybe he was right, but I'd have rather finished on my feet. I think I could have.

"You can't have a rainbow without rain," Turner said afterward.

Six months later, I fought the same guy again and won a decision.

My last amateur loss came just after I turned seventeen. I got caught early, came back to hurt the other guy, and wound up one point short in the scoring. "One more round and you would have knocked him out," Turner said.

I got good grades in high school. I had an active social life. There were no fights outside the gym.

In March of my senior year, I made it to the finals of the New York Metropolitan Area Golden Gloves. The opponent, fresh out of a year in Rahway State Prison, was Johnny Bruton.

Turner knew what had happened between us. In the dressing room before the fight, he sat me down for a talk.

"This isn't about going crazy," he said. "It's about winning the fight. You've beaten fighters with better skills than this guy has. But maybe he's inside your head a little because he broke your nose four years ago. Get over it. Control your emotions. And do not let him intimidate you. I want you to punch him in the face with your jab all night long."

When the ring announcer introduced us before the fight, Bruton touched the tip of his nose with his glove. There was a mean look in his eyes.

The bell rang and it was just the two of us.

I controlled round one with my jab. In round two, Bruton made some adjustments.

"This guy has started moving his head to his left instead of to the right to avoid your jab," Turner told me after the second round. "That brings him directly into your righthand power alley. Feint with the jab. And if he moves to his left, crack him."

Round three. I feinted with my jab. Bruton moved his head to his left, and I fired a righthand with everything I could put on it. It landed, flush on his jaw.

He wobbled. The referee was slow coming in.

What happened next came from four years of training and a hunger for revenge. I followed with my best shot. Another righthand that landed squarely on Bruton's nose. I felt the bone give. He crumpled to the canvas. Every sacrifice made, every hour spent in the gym, every punch I'd taken for four years was worthwhile.

The next day, Turner sat me down on the same bench we'd sat on when I first came to the gym. "I saw some mean in you last night," he said. "For a fighter, that's good. Now there's something I want to talk with you about."

I waited.

"Last night, you got what you came here for. This guy, Johnny Bruton, broke your nose. So you put him in the hospital and broke his nose back. Now you've got to decide what happens next. You're good. Maybe you can be something in boxing. Make good money someday as a pro. But you're a smart young man and you have other options. So the question is whether turning pro at some time in the future is in your thoughts. If it is, we'll plan accordingly."

I said I was interested.

"Then we'll take things to the next level," Turner told me.

Two weeks later, an ex-fighter named Robby Aiken came to the gym. Robby had been a promising middleweight until a bad shoulder forced him out of the ring. After a year in limbo, he'd taken up training. Five years later, he'd developed a reputation for being bullheaded, opinionated, and a very good trainer.

The deal that Turner made with Robby was simple. Robby could use the gym free of charge to work with his own fighters. In exchange, he'd help train me. "This guy knows pro boxing better than I do," Turner told me. "Both of us can learn from him."

Three months later, I graduated from high school. I needed a lawyer if I was going to turn pro.

"Ask Jerry," Turner suggested.

So Banana-Brain went to Izzy for advice, and Izzy referred me to Craig Meyers.

Craig was a large broad-shouldered man; forty-five years old with a shaved head and deep booming voice. He was making enough money as a litigator to live in a million-dollar house in Englewood Cliffs. Just as important, he was a boxing fan with a keen understanding of the business.

"Jerry says I should be good to you," Craig told me when we met at his office. "So I'll make a deal with you. Fighting is a risky business. It's speculative at best; you need something to fall back on. So here's the deal. You turn pro now, but you also go to college. You take at least twenty credits a year, which will put you on track to graduate in six years. You take real courses; no yoga or basket-weaving or bullshit like that. You give me two tickets ringside for every one of your fights. And I'll do your legal work for free."

"What's in it for you? Two tickets are two tickets."

"I like feeling good about myself," Craig said. "And thirty-five years ago, I was one of Jerry's kids."

That summer, I had my first pro fight on a club card at the Robert Treat Hotel in Newark. Undercard dressing rooms are quiet places. Music is rare and voices are muted. Turner gloved me up and looked on as Robby worked the pads with me until I was loose. Then we left for the ring.

The opponent was a guy named Danny Sullivan, who was making his pro debut too. The great John L. he wasn't. He'd only had eight amateur bouts and didn't know how to fight. I kept stuffing my jab in his face.

"Danny; keep your hands up," one of his cornermen shouted. So Danny raised his hands like someone taking a course in how to box by the numbers, and I slammed a hook into his body.

"Danny Sullivan KO 1" is the first entry beneath my name in the record book.

In late August, I started college. My courses were in the morning. I did roadwork and other physical conditioning before class and was in the gym every weekday afternoon.

Turner was in charge of my training, but Robby played an ever-expanding role. Robby also took it upon himself to shut down any over-confidence that might be lurking in my psyche.

"If you think you're gonna make it to the bigtime in a hurry, forget about it," he said after I knocked out Danny Sullivan. That was followed by, "You think that a fighter is only as good as his last fight. But you're wrong. A fighter is only as good as the fight he's in now. You have to prove yourself every time."

Robby could be a pain in the ass, but he was innovative and technically sound. I give him credit for a lot of things and one thing in particular. He knew more about certain aspects of boxing than Turner did. But he always respected Turner's role and never once did anything to undermine him.

Robby also doubled as my cutman during fights; although fortunately, I didn't need those services for anything more serious than reducing some swelling around my eyes.

Craig did my legal work for free and, as it turned out, handled the managerial chores too. In my first year as a pro, I had six fights; all of them against opponents who weren't very good. I fought guys who, before the fight, had faces that looked like the after. It's a wonder that some of them were licensed to box by the state athletic commission. But that's the way boxing is. Prospects feed on bums at the start.

I had fast hands, a good jab, and my righthand was capable of doing damage. If an opponent got in close, I could hurt him with a hook to the body. And I had a chin.

"Either a fighter has a chin or he doesn't," Turner said. "It's there or it isn't. Your whiskers are good."

After two years, my record was 12-and-0 with 7 knockouts. The competition was getting tougher and the purses were getting bigger. People thought I was good-looking. And when it came to selling tickets, it didn't hurt that I was white. For my first pro fight, I'd been paid $1,500. Fight number thirteen, against a journeyman named Lorenzo Crawford, paid me $20,000. That's a lot of money in boxing. But I was putting asses in seats.

Fight number thirteen also saw me knocked on my ass. Crawford caught me with a hook up top that buzzed me. Holding on and tying your opponent up when you're hurt is easier said than done. He whacked me again and I went down.

I knew where I was. I got up.

"He's going to keep doing what he's doing until you make him stop," Turner told me between rounds. "All he has is the hook. Keep your right hand close to your temple to protect yourself. Move laterally and re-establish your jab."

It wasn't my finest hour, but I won a decision. Then, instead of putting me in soft on the chance that getting knocked down had damaged my confidence, Turner stepped up the competition. I responded by winning my next fight on a sixth-round knockout.

Ten per cent of each purse went to Turner as his trainer's fee. It was one of the few times in his life that he'd made halfway decent money from training a fighter. And I was blessed. I didn't have to pay the typical thirty percent manager's fee.

"You save your money," Craig instructed. "I'm not doing this so you can go out and buy bling and piss it all away on good times that don't mean a thing."

I listened. I'd never had money before and saved what I could. I was still living with Catherine Cerabone. After I turned pro, I gave her five hundred dollars each month for rent. The only jewelry I owned was a four-hundred-dollar watch and a necklace I'd won in the Golden Gloves.

In my fifteenth pro fight, I went ten rounds for the first time in my career and won a unanimous decision.

Then I knocked out a pretty good prospect in a sold-out ballroom in Atlantic City. That paid $30,000, the biggest purse I'd earned so far.

Craig started teaching me about tax-free municipal bonds and the difference between safe investments and risky ones. "Anyone who tells you that they can double your money can lose all of it," he cautioned.

Meanwhile, I'd been working hard in the gym and in school. Turner decided to give me a breather. Fight number seventeen was a step down in the quality of opposition.

"Don't get cocky," Robby warned in the dressing room before the fight. "Any fighter in any fight is just one punch away from being knocked out."

So I was careful; although I'm not sure that getting in a boxing ring to have a professional fighter throw punches at you can ever be considered careful. I waited until the end of round one when I saw an opening and staggered Horace Gibbs (the ex-con from Cleveland with bulging muscles) with a good righthand. In round two, I knocked him out.

Four days later, I drove over to Craig's house in Englewood Cliffs to pick up my check. I was feeling pretty good about myself. I was twenty-one years old, halfway toward my college degree, and an undefeated professional fighter.

Not everything in my life was perfect. From time to time, I was aware of a loneliness inside me. I was still coming to grips with the fact that, despite everything Catherine Cerabone had tried to give me, I'd spent most of my childhood in an unhappy home. Still, life was good.

It was a nice day. Bright blue sky, seventy degrees, a gentle breeze. I decided to eat lunch in the park.

And then the most beautiful woman I'd ever seen materialized on the sidewalk in front of me, looked into my eyes, and said, "You're the fighter."

Part Two

How do you respond when a woman who's more beautiful than any fantasy you've ever had comes up to you on the street and says, "You're the fighter."

"That's one way of defining me," I said.

She smiled.

"What's your name?"

"Melissa."

Her smile was as pretty as the rest of her.

I extended my hand.

"Hello, Melissa."

The conversation flowed from there.

Melissa lived in Fort Lee, less than a mile from Englewood Cliffs. She was twenty-one, had a two-year community college degree, and was working as an administrator for a real-estate company. Four days earlier, a lawyer friend had taken her to her first pro fight. She'd liked the scene and loved the action. "Then you got in the ring and I held my breath," she said.

I asked if she'd had lunch. She hadn't. I bought a second sandwich and we went to the park. We walked and talked. Then she had to go back to work. I told her I'd like to see her again. We exchanged telephone numbers and made plans to have dinner on Friday night. I waited for Friday the way a six-year-old waits for Christmas.

Melissa lived in a high-rise apartment building two blocks from the Hudson River. I picked her up at seven o'clock and we went to an Italian restaurant. Afterward, we walked along a path overlooking the river.

A lot of the earlier conversation had been about boxing. Now it turned to family.

"What do your parents do?" she asked.

"I don't have parents."

I explained. And she took my hand.

Toward the end of the evening, I asked if she was involved with anyone.

"Not really," she said. "I've been dating someone, but it's not serious."

"Can I see you again?"

She had plans for Saturday and Sunday. But Monday, she was free for coffee after work.

We said goodnight outside her building.

"I had a nice time," she told me.

"Can I kiss you?"

"Yes."

So I kissed her. A gentle lingering kiss. And a jolt of electricity went through me.

On Monday, we had coffee, which morphed into dinner. Melissa was busy the rest of the week. "And I have family plans on the weekend," she said. "But I'll cook dinner for you a week from Saturday if you'd like."

I arrived for my home-cooked meal bearing flowers. Melissa's apartment had two bedrooms with a living room that looked out over the Manhattan skyline. Her roommate, a woman named Robin, was spending the night with her boyfriend.

Melissa explained over dinner that the lawyer she'd gone to the fights with was actually the guy she'd been dating. "I wasn't completely honest with you," she said. The "family business" she'd tended to the previous weekend was breaking up with him. "I don't like triangles," she told me. I took that as a promising sign.

After dinner, we sat in the living room. Melissa put on some music. A song that I'd never heard before was playing. A love song with a gentle rock beat:

There's something that I have to tell you.
There's something that I have to say.
You were right and I was wrong about love.

Melissa was looking at me with something wonderful in her eyes.

And then we were in each other's arms on a rapturous journey unlike any journey that I'd been on before. We kissed and touched and made love, and the pleasure kept escalating and went on and on until the volcano in each of us exploded at the same time.

"I guess we're sexually compatible," Melissa said as we lay in bed, fully spent. "But we knew that before tonight, didn't we."

Over the next few weeks, we spent every hour possible together. Melissa worked. I was busy in the gym and with school. Friday and Saturday were our nights together.

I'd never been in love before. And it occurred to me that Melissa might be falling in love too.

Then circumstances changed.

"Robin is moving out to live with her boyfriend," Melissa told me.

"How would you feel about my moving in?"

"I was hoping you'd ask that."

The first person I told was Catherine. Melissa and I took her to dinner. She was genuinely happy for us. "I owe you a lot," I said. "You've watched over me since I was born. You'll always be in my life."

Then I told Turner and Robby. Turner was fine with it all. Robby was less enthusiastic. "I just want to get one thing straight," he demanded. "Which means more to you; this woman or boxing?"

"Melissa."

"I don't care what her name is. Which means more to you; boxing or this Melissa?"

"I just told you. Melissa."

"Jesus; that's not what I want to hear."

Turner laughed.

"Look," I countered. "Which means more to you; your family or boxing?"

"That's different. They're my family."

"Well, I don't have a family."

That shut Robby up temporarily.

"Boxing and Melissa aren't mutually exclusive," I said. "I can do more than one thing right."

"Just to be safe," Turner suggested, "run it through Craig."

So Melissa and I had dinner with Craig.

"What can I say?" my lawyer-manager advised thereafter. "The first thing about her that reaches out and grabs you is that she's incredibly beautiful. And the next thing is that, unless I'm missing something, she's incredibly nice. Go for it. Just don't get her pregnant."

"We've had that conversation. At this point in our lives, neither of us want it. We're both careful."

That left Melissa's parents. Catherine was happier to meet Melissa than Melissa's parents were to meet me. Or phrased differently, a father and mother love it when their twenty-one-year-old daughter, who's smart, wonderful, breathtakingly beautiful, and dating a lawyer, announces that she's about to start living with a club fighter from Newark who she met six weeks ago.

With more than a little trepidation, I went with Melissa to her parents' home for dinner.

32

"I've been thinking," I said as we approached the front door. "After getting beat on in seventeen professional fights, how bad can this be?"

"Don't worry," she assured me. "Whatever they say, we're living together."

By the end of the evening, I had the feeling that Melissa's mother kind of liked me. And her father was weakening a bit.

"Are you sure you want to do this?" he asked his daughter.

"I've never been more certain of anything in my life."

Two months after Melissa and I met, I moved all of my worldly possessions into her apartment. There wasn't much. In the course of a day, we brought everything in, unpacked the cartons, and converted the second bedroom into a study.

My mother's photograph had been in the bottom drawer of my bureau for a decade. Now I put it on a corner of my desk. For the first time since I was four years old, I felt like I had a home.

That night, I sat Melissa down on the bed. "I don't know if I can put into words how happy I am to be here," I said. "I don't want to do anything that upsets you, ever. If I screw up, tell me, and I'll try to make it right."

I wouldn't have changed places with anyone in the world.

Part Three

Three weeks after Melissa and I started living together, I had my next fight.

"You've looked good in the gym lately," Turner told me several days before the bout.

"I've felt good," I said.

The opponent was a 16-and-2 heavyweight from South Carolina. Sixteen-and-two from South Carolina is like 8-and-10 from New York. I knocked him out in four rounds.

Melissa was sitting at ringside with Craig. It was the first time she'd seen me fight since we'd known each other. "There were some anxious moments," she admitted afterward. "But I can handle it."

Every day was a bit sunnier because Melissa was in my life. Nights were different from what I'd known before. Over the years, I'd slept fitfully. It was common for me to toss and turn and wake up several times. With Melissa beside me, I slept peacefully.

We shared the household chores like cleaning, marketing, and laundry. I was making good money and wanted to pay the entire rent on the apartment, but Melissa insisted on paying half. Each month, I sent Catherine Cerabone a check for five hundred dollars. I thought it was the right thing to do.

After I beat Mr South Carolina, I took a week off from the gym. Then I went back to work. Once serious training resumed, Melissa asked if she could come to the gym to watch me spar.

Turner doesn't like people hanging around the gym. "Factory workers don't bring their friends to the assembly line," he says from time to time. But he told me it was all right.

So Melissa came to the gym. Generally, she dresses down. People still notice. It's hard not to if you have eyes. Whatever she wears, she looks better in it than anyone else.

Robby was less than enthralled by her presence.

I was scheduled to spar three rounds with a Philadelphia heavyweight named Cooper Hitchens. Robby was overseeing the session and, after three rounds, suggested we go one more. I said fine. Then I saw Robby saying something real quiet-like in Hitchens's ear.

Hitchens started the fourth round of sparring like he'd boxed the first three. Then, a minute in when nothing much was happening, he threw a righthand with knockout on it. You don't do that in sparring unless it's understood in advance that you'll be going hard. I saw it coming, moved my head to the side, and fired back with a hard counter right.

Boom! Hitchens wobbled.

"Time!" Robby called. Then he was in my face.

"What are you doing; showing off for your girlfriend?"

I gave him a dirty look.

"I asked you a question. Are you showing off for this girl you brought to the gym?"

"You told Hitchens to cheap-shot me because I brought Melissa to the gym."

"That's crazy."

"Don't bullshit me, Robby. You're always talking

39

about how important it is to be honest. I know what happened. You were trying to show me up."

"We're done for the day. Go take a shower."

I turned toward the shower area.

"Wait a minute," a voice from behind said.

I stopped.

"You did good work in there today," Robby told me. "Especially that last round."

That night, Melissa and I had dinner with friends. The following evening, we watched *World Championship Boxing* on HBO.

"How long do you think you'll fight?" Melissa asked before the telecast began.

"I don't know. I started boxing because I was angry. I liked it, and I liked being good. Then I realized I could make some money. It's not who I am, but it's what I'm doing for now. Besides," I added, "without boxing and your coming to the fights that night, I wouldn't have met you."

The HBO telecast wasn't just any fight. Boxing goes through cycles that are tied to the heavyweight division. With great fanfare, the sweet science had entered the Carver Boyd era.

The media was fond of saying that Boyd came out

of nowhere. Actually, he came out of a prison in Texas, where he'd done four years for beating up a hooker so badly that she died. After his release, he was indicted again; this time for pummelling a stripper beyond recognition. On the eve of trial, she disappeared and the case was dismissed.

Boyd's promoter was Vernon Jack, who'd made his mark in the shady world where rap music and finance intersect. Earlier in Jack's life, he'd been one of the largest numbers operators in Detroit.

Carver Boyd unified the heavyweight championship by going through the division like a meat cleaver through strawberry shortcake. At five-eleven, 220 pounds, he was a shade larger than Mike Tyson. Like Tyson, he fought with savage fury, using a bob-and-weave method of defense and attack.

Watching Boyd fight was like watching a pitbull tear a rabbit apart. Early in his career, one opponent went six rounds with him. Everyone else got knocked out.

Boyd wore black sequined trunks in the ring. A swastika was tattooed on his left biceps because, in his words, "I'm a killer and a technician." After Boyd won the heavyweight title, his antisocial behavior continued. There were misogynistic, anti-white, homophobic tirades and lewd public behavior. He was a regular in the private rooms at adult clubs. The word on the street was that there'd been at least one incident involving a twelve-year-old boy.

"The best thing about being a fighter," Boyd declared, "is being able to smash someone's face in and get paid for it." He openly wondered what it would be like to kill an opponent in the ring. Fighters, good fighters, went in against him scared. Not the normal fear that fighters feel; something more.

Like Mike Tyson before him, Boyd had entered the national consciousness. HBO went gaga over him. His opponent on the night that Melissa and I watched him together for the first time was Alexander Parchuk, a pretty good heavyweight from Russia who didn't stand a chance. It ended brutally in round two, with Parchuk unconscious on the canvas and blood streaming from his mouth.

"To prepare for Carver Boyd," HBO analyst Larry Merchant advised the audience in his end-of-telecast commentary, "a fighter should spar with a tank that's firing live ammunition."

"I'm the baddest motherfucker in the world," Boyd told Merchant. "Anything I want, I take."

"Thank God, you're not fighting him," Melissa told me.

"Don't be so sure," I said.

A fighter is always on the edge. Everything makes a difference; every little detail counts. One punch can send years of hard work swirling down the drain. No matter how conscientiously I prepared for each fight, there were always people on the other side trying to screw everything up for me.

As my career progressed, Craig made the decision to forgo signing me to a long-term contract with a promoter. As long as I brought in paying customers and stayed undefeated, we had the leverage to stay independent. People were starting to whisper in my ear that a big-time manager could help me more. I told them, "Thanks, but no thanks."

Over the next few years, I fought for a half-dozen different promoters. I was on the undercard of a championship fight at Madison Square Garden. Then I went to Las Vegas and fought on the undercard of a big pay-per-view event. "It will be good exposure," Craig told me. "And I'd like you to get a feel for Vegas. With luck, you'll be fighting there someday for a lot of money."

I kept winning. By the time I turned twenty-four, my record was 28-and-0 with 13 knockouts. I hadn't fought particularly formidable opposition; mostly club fighters and a few once-world-class guys who were past their prime. Then I was matched against Toby Carter; a 17-and-0 heavyweight out of Dallas.

Carter could punch. He had sixteen knockouts. But his record had been built against guys softer than the ones I'd fought. And he had trouble taking a punch, which is a serious liability for a heavyweight. After I knocked him down for the third time, the ring doctor asked him if he knew where he was and Toby answered, "Dallas-Fort Worth International Airport." That wasn't the answer the doctor had in mind, since we were at a casino in Connecticut at the time. The fight was stopped.

Meanwhile, Turner and I decided that Robby was making enough of a contribution that he should get more than free gym privileges for his efforts. Since I wasn't paying a manager, I started giving him two per cent out of each purse on top of the ten per cent that I was paying to Turner.

44

Melissa and I were still happy together. People said that we made a nice-looking couple, and her parents had come around to liking me. With her help, I was losing some of my rough edges. I'm embarrassed to say this. But before we met, I hadn't known how to properly use a knife and fork. I'd cut my meat with the knife in my left hand, so I didn't have to switch hands before lifting the fork to my mouth.

"That's the old European way," she said gently. Under her tutelage, I became a modern American diner.

I asked Melissa once, "Why are you with me? You could have an easy life with any man you wanted."

"I've been with men who had money," she said. "Successful businessmen, good-looking, even nice. And I wasn't happy. You turn me on. Being with you makes me feel good about myself. And outside the ring, you're the nicest man I know."

Anywhere we went, I felt good about being with her. One time, we were invited to a wedding. Her former roommate, Robin, was getting married. Melissa was the maid of honor.

"When are you two getting hitched?" Robin asked after she and her husband had taken their vows.

"Someday," I told her.

The only sour note of the day came from Robin's cousin. Roderick had a graduate business degree and worked in marketing for an insurance company. He was snotty and condescending; the kind of guy you hope will get eaten by a mutant crocodile at the end of a grade-B horror movie.

Melissa and I were seated for dinner at the same table as Roderick. He began the conversation by telling us about a one-man play he'd gone to at a local theater. It was awful. Roderick wanted to leave, but there were only four people in the audience and his date insisted that they wait until intermission. Then they went to a restaurant next door for something to eat. After they sat down, the other two people from the audience came in.

Roderick thought it was hilarious that, when the actor went onstage for Act Two, there would be no one in the audience.

I felt sorry for the actor.

Roderick was taken with Melissa and openly disdainful toward me. He made several plays for her attention, was rebuffed, and decided to push my buttons instead.

46

"Robin tells me that you get punched in the head for a living."

"Only when I can't avoid the punches."

"What's it like getting punched in the head?"

"I'll show you."

Actually, I didn't say that. I know his type. They look down on fighters. Cops too, unless they've been mugged and need help. They also think that anyone who joins the armed forces is stupid, although they pretend to care deeply about our troops overseas. I try not to sink to their level.

"It hurts," I answered.

"What good books have you read lately?"

The question and tone of voice that accompanied it suggested I didn't, or couldn't, read.

Then Melissa got into the act, making it clear whose side she was on.

"The last book Roderick read was *The Poky Little Puppy*," she offered.

At which point, Robin's nine-year-old nephew approached our table and asked for my autograph, reaffirming the view that, to some, being a fighter is an honored profession.

47

Three months after my twenty-fourth birthday, I graduated from college. At 220 pounds, I was thirty pounds heavier than Jack Dempsey and Rocky Marciano, ten pounds heavier than Joe Louis. In today's world, that made me a "small" heavyweight; but I figured I was big enough. Carver Boyd weighed 220 pounds, and he was boxing's gold standard.

In the heavyweight division, there was Boyd and everyone else.

In August, I took a big step forward. Tashard Logan, a former Olympian, had an *HBO Boxing After Dark* date in Atlantic City. His promoter needed an opponent who was acceptable to HBO. He knew I could sell tickets and figured that Logan would beat me. My purse was $175,000; far more than I'd ever earned for a fight.

Logan was the first world-class fighter I'd faced. At the start of training, Robby suggested that I stop sleeping with Melissa until after the fight. Not just eliminate the sex; stop sleeping together altogether.

"I sleep better when I'm with her," I said.

"So far, things have worked out fine the way they are," Turner decreed when Robby raised the issue with him. "Why change? Besides; it's not the sex that kills them. It's the chase."

48

I won every round of my first fight on HBO en route to a 100–90, 100–90, 99–91 decision. "Technically, he's a good fighter," Logan said of me during the post-fight interview. "He doesn't give you much to work with."

Afterward, Turner gave me hell. "This is a guy you should have knocked out in five or six rounds," he said. "You let him hang around all night. You're fighting at a world-class level now. You've got to set down on your punches and put some hurt on people or they're going to put hurt on you. That doesn't mean be reckless. But you have to trust your instincts and take chances."

Be that as it may, the powers that be at HBO were impressed. A week after Thanksgiving, I was back on the network fighting Carmine LaGuardia. "You're in the money now," Craig told me when the contract was signed. "Four hundred thousand dollars."

LaGuardia was a big heavyweight; six feet five inches, 245 pounds. His record was comparable to mine but with more knockouts. Two of the world sanctioning organizations rated him in the top ten.

At the pre-fight physical, the examining doctor asked me to recite the months of the year backwards.

49

I guess that costs the state less money than a CT-scan or MRI.

"December . . . November . . . October . . . September . . . August . . . July . . . June . . . May . . . April . . . March . . . February . . . Purple."

"That's a joke," I added. But the doctor wasn't listening.

The LaGuardia fight was scheduled for twelve rounds. It lasted five. I was better than I'd ever been before.

Negotiations for my next fight began. Several potential opponents were in the mix; the most likely being a German heavyweight named Bruno Gloeck, who was ranked sixth by the World Boxing Council and ninth by the International Boxing Federation.

Two weeks before Christmas, Craig called. "Turner and I want to meet with you at my office," he said. "Something interesting has come up."

An hour later, I was sitting with Turner and Craig in a conference room overlooking northern New Jersey. Craig skipped the small talk and got to the point.

"We have an offer for you to fight Carver Boyd."

Silence.

"How much?" I asked.

"A million dollars. But that's a starting point for negotiations. They'll go higher."

"Tell me more."

"They're looking at April 4th at the MGM Grand in Las Vegas. HBO will televise it."

"Carver Boyd would be the best fighter you've ever fought," Turner offered. "Probably the best you ever will. But there's areas where you match up well against him. Whether you win depends on how you perform on the night of the fight. Boyd intimidates people before they get in the ring, and they don't perform the way they should."

"What do I do to win?"

Turner smiled. "We'll get to that. The first thing is to make sure you want the fight."

"Yes; if the money is right."

"How much is right?"

"That's up to Craig. And one thing more; no options. I'm not signing my career over to Vernon Jack."

"That's a problem," Craig said. "Jack will insist on options."

"Then there won't be a fight. I know what the deal

is. I'm the next sacrificial lamb for Carver Boyd. If I win, we're taking home all the marbles."

"I'll see what I can do," Craig promised.

Melissa wasn't happy when I recounted the day's events. Carver Boyd terrified her. But she understood where I was coming from. "Football players want to play in the Super Bowl," I told her. "A fighter wants to fight for the heavyweight championship of the world."

Christmas came and went. The negotiations moved forward. Vernon Jack raised his offer to $1,500,000 plus a non-refundable $50,000 that would be designated as training expenses. Then Craig went to war over the sanctioning fees that would be paid to the world sanctioning organizations. All four of the major belts would be on the line. "But we're not paying more than a total of three per cent," he told Jack. "If you don't like it, find someone else for Carver Boyd to beat up on."

Jack agreed that no more than $45,000 would be deducted from my purse for sanctioning fees. Anything more would come out of someone else's pocket. Clearly, he wanted me as the opponent.

The parameters of the contract took shape. My purse would be $1,500,000 backed by a letter of credit drawn on a federal reserve bank no later than twenty-one days prior to the fight. The $50,000 styled as training expenses would be paid in advance. The sanctioning fees deducted from my purse would be capped at $45,000. I'd be required to attend one kick-off press conference in New York and one fight-week press conference in Las Vegas. The referee and judges would be appointed by the Nevada State Athletic Commission, with either fighter's camp having the right to object to the appointment of any official for good cause subject to the rules of the commission. There would be first-class plane tickets to and from Las Vegas for Turner, Craig, Robby, Melissa, and myself; and hotel accommodations at the MGM Grand for Melissa and myself (a two-bedroom suite), Turner (a one-bedroom suite), Craig (a one-bedroom suite), and Robby (a standard room). A private gym with a regulation-size ring would be available at all times during fight week. We'd have limousine service and daily food allowances of two hundred dollars per person. Craig and Melissa would be given first-row tickets.

A kick-off press conference was tentatively scheduled for January 15th at the Rainbow Room in

Manhattan. But the options were still a problem. Vernon Jack sent Craig a "final contract." Everything was in order except for a provision that read, "In the event Challenger wins the fight, Promoter shall have the exclusive right to promote his next six bouts pursuant to the following terms and conditions."

The "following terms and conditions" were draconian. The contract remained unsigned.

"No signed contract, no press conference," Craig told Jack. "We're not crossing the Hudson River without a contract, and the contract will not have options."

Jack figured we were bluffing. On January 12th, the media was invited to a kick-off press conference three days hence for "boxing's next mega-fight."

Craig and I caucused. "If you're game," he said, "this is how we handle it."

On January 15th, Turner, Craig, Robby, Melissa, and I drove into Manhattan. We arrived at Rockefeller Center shortly before noon and were escorted upstairs. The Rainbow Room was jammed with media personnel and television cameras. We waited in a lounge overlooking Fifth Avenue. Then the festivities began.

After everyone else was seated at the dais, Carver Boyd and I entered the room simultaneously as per Vernon Jack's stage instructions.

Boyd's face seethed with hate.

Jack began the proceedings. "Today is Martin Luther King Jr's birthday," he solemnly intoned. "And this fight will take place on the anniversary of a tragic event in American history. On April 4th, 1968, the great courageous and beloved Reverend Martin Luther King Jr was assassinated. Dr King fought his entire life to ensure that all oppressed minorities could compete with the majority on a level playing field. And one thing that we all know about boxing is that, inside the ring, the playing field is level. We also know that Carver Boyd is a dynamic example of the proud black men and women that Dr King envisioned in his dream."

Over the next half-hour, the promoter introduced a representative of the MGM Grand, rambled on about several sponsors, and called Carver Boyd "the greatest heavyweight of our time and perhaps all time." I was referenced as "a young man from New Jersey who wants to become the heavywhite champion of the world."

Then it was time for Craig, as my "manager," to speak.

"Does everybody have their pens ready and cameras rolling?" he asked as he took the microphone. "Good. Because we're going to find out in the next two minutes whether this fight is happening or not."

There were puzzled looks around the room.

"Vernon Jack and I have spent a month negotiating the fight contract," Craig said. "We're in agreement on everything with one exception. Our side will not – I repeat; we will not – sign a contract with an option clause. I've voiced that position again and again in negotiations with Vernon. I've sent a dozen emails to his attorney stating our position with regard to options. He can't claim that what I'm saying now is a surprise."

Craig held up three documents.

"These are copies of the bout contract that Vernon sent to me for signing. I've made one change in the contract. I've crossed out the option clause."

Craig handed the contracts to me and I signed each one with a flourish.

"All right," he continued. "We've shown you all that we're ready to fight Carver Boyd with everything on the line. The question now is whether Carver Boyd and his promoter are afraid of the fight."

"Fuck you," Vernon Jack said.

"What's the matter, Vernon? Don't you believe in your fighter?"

"Ain't got nothing to do with believing in my fighter."

"Sure, it does. Options are only relevant if your guy loses. You aren't hedging your bets, are you?"

"You're wasting your breath," Jack responded.

"Either you sign this contact now or we walk out of the room and there's no fight."

"Pull this shit with me and you'll never get a fight with Carver Boyd."

"The only problem I see is that maybe big bad Carver Boyd is afraid of the fight. What do you say, Carver? Are you looking for a way out?"

Boyd turned to his promoter. "Sign the contract," he said.

Now the dialogue was between Vernon Jack and his fighter.

"Champ; you don't understand—"

"You don't need options. I'll beat this white boy to a pulp."

"Champ; the way we do things in this business—"

Boyd's next words were spoken with the threat of

physical violence implicit in his body language and tone of voice.

"Sign the fucking contract."

It was high drama. Vernon Jack weighed his choices. Then, very deliberately, he reached into his jacket pocket, took out a pen, signed all three copies of the contract, and handed one back to Craig.

The proceedings resumed.

"We know what we're up against," Turner said when it was his turn at the microphone. "Guys like Sonny Liston and Mike Tyson come along, and people think they're Godzilla. No one can beat them. They're gonna be champion for a thousand years. And then someone beats them."

"Muhammad Ali beat Sonny Liston," Jack interrupted. "Is your guy as good as Muhammad Ali?"

"Maybe not. But he's as good as Buster Douglas. And we all know what Buster did to Tyson."

I didn't say much when it was my turn to speak; just that this was a great opportunity and I was looking forward to the fight. That sounded a bit weak, so I added, "I know what Carver Boyd brings to the table. I'll deal with it."

Boyd began his remarks by suggesting that I bring

a paramedic, not a cutman, to Las Vegas and closed with, "This fight is on the anniversary of an assassination, but it will be an execution."

Then it was time for the ritual staredown. Carver Boyd and I moved in front of the podium and stood facing each other nose-to-nose. I was four inches taller than he was. In that moment, height seemed my only physical advantage.

"The fight starts now," I told myself.

I stared into Boyd's eyes, blocking out everything else. I always do it that way. It reduces the opponent to a pair of eyes and gives mine a deadened killer look.

"You don't want to fuck with me," Boyd said.

I ignored him.

"I'm going to smash your pretty-boy face until all anyone sees is pieces of bone and blood. When you get in the ring with me, there's gonna be a sign in flashing lights that says *your brain bleeds tonight*."

Part Four

The day after the kick-off press conference, Turner sat me down in the gym. "We've got ten weeks," he said. "And then another week in Vegas. Every hour of that time is important, so here's the plan."

"You've always matched up well against smaller guys, and Boyd is shorter than you are. He's a big puncher, but the key to his effectiveness is his quickness. He has the fastest delivery of any hard puncher ever, except maybe Mike Tyson and Joe Louis. You're as quick on the trigger as he is and your hands are just as fast. He's not used to that."

"Boyd is a smart fighter. He doesn't just throw punches. He knows how to place them. He throws lights-out punches with both hands, and his hook to the body can break a man physically and mentally."

"Most guys go out to fight Carver Boyd; and they're so intimidated that they say to themselves, 'Let me just try to survive for five or six rounds. Then maybe he'll get tired and I can do something with him.' You can't fight Carver Boyd like that. If all you try to do is survive, he'll track you down, beat you up, and knock you out. Most guys do one of two things against him. Either they freeze up or they run. If you freeze, he'll knock you out in ninety seconds. If you run, it might take him a few rounds."

"The best way to survive against Boyd is to try to beat him. You're going to fight this guy. You've got to throw punches. That doesn't mean standing there and going toe-to-toe. But you're going to fight with him."

"You cannot back up. If you back up, you're dead meat. You cannot beat Carver Boyd going backwards. And don't think you can dance around the ring and throw dipshit jabs to keep him off, because you can't. You have to throw a good hard jab. You stuff your jab in his motherfucking face and stop him in his tracks. And you do it all night. Anytime you're in range, you get off first. Boyd can throw off either foot. But he can't throw going backwards and he has to set himself to punch."

"If you stand in front of Boyd, he'll hurt you. If you let him come right at you, he'll hurt you. You keep him busy. And you do that by being aggressive; not reckless but aggressive. You've got to fight smart and not make mistakes, and you've got to be tough when the time comes that you need it."

"This is a fist-fight; the man's going to hit you. What matters is how hard, how often, and how you respond when he does. It's a twelve-round fight. You've never gone twelve rounds before, but neither has Boyd. You've gone ten rounds five times. Boyd has never gone past eight. You're gonna be more ready to fight twelve rounds than he is. You take no rounds off. You fight this motherfucker all night long. I want those late rounds to belong to you. We'll see how tough he is late."

Robby was more active than in the past where the day-to-day mechanics of preparing me to fight were concerned. Turner was relying on him for support, maybe even guidance. And he delivered.

I'd never done much padwork in the gym.

Turner once told me, "It doesn't make sense for a trainer to put big mittens on his hands, stand in front of his fighter, and tell his fighter to punch the mittens."

But preparing for Boyd, Turner had Robby on the pads with me, simulating Boyd's style, bobbing and weaving for a half-hour at the start of each session.

"Boyd moves three times to get inside his opponent's jab," Robby explained. "He moves to his left, then the right, then left again and he hooks. He does it fast. And he doesn't just move his head from side to side. When he moves his head to the side, he dips down so it goes from right to left and left to right in an arc. He's short and the dip makes him shorter. When Boyd sets up, you hit him fast. A jab to the shoulder; something, anything, that beats him to the punch. If he's standing still, you can jab at his face. If he's coming forward doing a bob and weave, go for his collarbone. If you hit him in the collarbone with a stiff jab, it will force him to reset. And if you aim for the collarbone, maybe you'll hit him in the face. That's better than aiming for his face, missing high, and having him counter."

Day after day, hour after hour, Robby simulated

the bob and weave with me on the pads. It got so the rhythm was in my mind every night when I went to sleep, which was what Turner wanted.

When we reached the point where it was time for me to spar, Turner brought in four sparring partners. The best of them was a journeyman from Mexico. Reynoldo Cortez didn't have much of a punch. But he was built like Carver Boyd and fought with the same rhythm and bob-and-weave style.

The sparring sessions were hard. The sparring partners were instructed to come forward with all-out aggression; just like Boyd. And they alternated rounds, so they were always fresh.

The cardinal rule drummed into my head before each session was Don't Back Up. "You throw your jab; you throw righthands; you do anything," Turner instructed. "But you do not back up. If a buzz-saw is coming at you, you get out of the way by moving to the side or you jam up the works, which is a jab in the face. You don't back up because, if you do, the buzz-saw will cut you in half."

Training for Boyd, if I backed up during a round, Turner would call "time" and reset the three-minute clock. Then the round started all over again.

In early March, at Vernon Jack's request, we opened the gym for a "media day." I went through a light workout and sparred two rounds. "Today, you back up," Robby instructed beforehand. "Let all these reporters get the wrong idea. Just don't develop any bad habits."

Afterward, we sat with a group of writers. "To beat Carver Boyd," I said, "you need a good jab, a fast righthand; and when he hits you, you have to be able to take the punch. The last part is the hard part."

An Internet blogger asked what it was like for "a white guy from Newark to get in the ring with all these angry black fighters."

"Every opponent gives me grief," I said. "It's not about color. The angry white guys and the angry black guys and the guys who fight clever and the guys who go for broke with every shot are all trying to punch me in the face."

"In forty-four fights," another reporter pressed, "Carver Boyd has never been knocked down. How do you feel about that?"

"If he gets knocked down, it will be interesting to see if he gets back up."

Near the end of the session, Turner offered the

thought that, outside the ring, I was a nice guy. But when the bell rang, I was a nasty son-of-a-bitch.

At the end of media day, it was clear that those in attendance thought that (a) I was a nice guy and (b) I had no chance.

Typically, a fighter leaves home and goes to training camp to prepare for a big fight. Defying conventional wisdom, I stayed put. I was comfortable living in Fort Lee with Melissa. And while a lot of people were stopping me on the street to wish me luck, we constructed a world that minimized distractions.

Melissa felt the pressure as much as I did. That highlight reel of Carver Boyd's is intimidating.

"Look at it this way," I told her. "I'm getting a million-and-a-half dollars. When the fight is over, after Turner and Robby are paid, after taxes, after everything else, we'll have seven hundred thousand dollars. Plus what I've saved from my earlier fights. That's not a bad start on life. And if I win, the sky's the limit."

"I just don't want you to get hurt," she said.

"That's a vote of confidence."

Bottom line: Being with Melissa kept me sane. I'm not sure I would have gotten through those ten weeks without her. Every time I looked at her, I told myself, "Whatever happens on April 4th, life is good."

Still, there was a lot of pressure. I felt it most at night when I was trying to fall asleep. Carver Boyd kept running through my head.

I'd lie in bed. Visualizing the fight made it harder to sleep, so I'd fast-forward in my mind to what would come afterward.

Growing up, I'd daydreamed about being a champion. All fighters do. Now that dream was one fight away from becoming reality.

After I beat Carver Boyd, I told myself, I'd be on everyone's A-list. I'd get a lot of attention. But the core of my life wouldn't change.

I'd stay in the same gym with the same people who brought me to the dance. If someone asked why the heavyweight champion of the world was training in a dilapidated gym in a neighborhood that urban renewal had left behind, I'd tell them, "If it ain't broke, don't fix it. So far, things are working out fine."

Turner would be happy. For both of us.

I couldn't imagine loving anyone as much as I loved Melissa. We'd share the rewards that came with my being champion.

The sound of Melissa's breathing as she slept comforted me at night. Then Carver Boyd would intrude on the fantasies. He was always there; an ominous presence in my mind.

"I had a dream last night," I told Turner several days before training came to an end. "I was driving on the highway in a small car. And huge tractor-trailer trucks were hurtling toward me."

"How'd you make out?"

"None of the trucks hit me, but it was scary."

Turner gestured for me to sit on one of the benches beside him.

"You asked me once, the day we met, what I did wrong when I was young. And I said maybe someday I'd tell you. I saw a lot of guys like Carver Boyd in my old line of work."

I waited and he went on.

"When I was young, I was smarter than anyone else. At least, that's what I thought. I was a street hustler; a pimp with a string of women. I didn't know it, but I was a poor excuse for a human being. I disrespected other people, particularly women, and put them in harm's way. I saw guys like Carver Boyd all the time. Guys with little dicks and guys who couldn't get it up; guys who bought women because it made them feel strong. One of those guys beat one of my girls up. Then he cut her to pieces and she died. It felt like I'd killed her. The cops came in. I had a lawyer that made a deal for me, so I didn't do jail time. I testified against the psycho that killed her and saved my own sorry ass. After that, I vowed to set my life straight. Trust me; I know about guys like Carver Boyd. He's a big man as long as everything is going his way. But if you give him something to think about, his dick will shrink to the size of a clitoris."

We flew out to Las Vegas on the Sunday before the fight. First-class tickets with limousine pick-up at the airport and VIP check-in at the hotel. "Win on Saturday night and they won't be able to do enough for you," Craig told me. "Lose and they won't know your name."

Carver Boyd's face was everywhere. On the felt covers over the gaming tables, on fight posters, even on the electronic room keys.

The "smart" money was on Boyd. Most of the

other money was too. The odds at the MGM Grand Sports Book were 15-to-1 in his favor. My record was 31-and-0 with 15 knockouts. But Boyd had 43 knockouts in 44 fights; a dozen of them against world-class opponents. It was even money that the fight wouldn't go four rounds.

The final pre-fight press conference was scheduled for noon on Wednesday in the media center. That morning, Turner and I strategized as to how I should respond when I came face-to-face with Boyd.

"If you avoid him, he'll think you're scared," Turner counselled.

"So what do I do?"

"Look him in the eye."

"And what does he do?"

"I don't know. Either a staredown or something crazy or maybe he says hello."

"And I do what?"

The appointed hour came. As was the script in New York, Boyd and I entered the media center together. I walked past him, said, "Hello, Carver," and moved on in a dismissive way.

The press conference began with Vernon Jack proclaiming that God was looking over Carver Boyd and had given him the strength to smite all enemies, domestic and foreign.

Turner offered the thought that, yes, he thought I had a realistic chance to win. "Sometimes the bully beats you," he said. "And sometimes you beat the bully."

"Either I'll win or I'll lose," I said when it was my turn to speak. "I'd rather win."

Then it was Carver Boyd time. "I live to hurt people," he told the gathering. "The ring is my slaughter-house. You don't want to mess with me unless you're carrying some pretty big guns. An AK-47 might do the job."

"He said 'might.'" Vernon Jack interjected.

Boyd ranted on, growing more and more profane. Finally, a woman sitting in the front row decided that she'd had enough. "Why do you find it necessary to talk like that?" she demanded.

"Suck my cock, lady."

Things were getting ugly.

"I asked you a question. This is a sporting event. Why do you act like this?"

Boyd unzipped his fly.

"Shut the fuck up or I'll come down there and shoot my wad in your face."

Then he stormed out of the room.

"I guess impulse control isn't Carver's strong point," Craig said afterward. "If nothing else, you're the sentimental favorite."

Reading the newspapers the next day, it seemed like every writer in the country was rooting for me and none of them were picking me to win.

On Thursday afternoon, Boyd and I weighed in. Normally, the weigh-in for a big event is held on Friday, the day before the fight. But with heavyweights, the scales are a formality.

Vernon Jack was maximizing every aspect of the promotion. The weigh-in was open to the public and conducted on a platform in the MGM Grand Garden Arena. Six thousand fans were there; most of them to see Carver Boyd. Melissa and Craig were seated in a guest area in the first row of the stands.

"Ladies and gentlemen . . . The challenger . . ."

I walked up the stairs to the platform with Turner and Robby at my side. Vernon Jack was standing by the scale with a representative of the Nevada State Athletic Commission.

"And now, making his way to the stage, the undisputed heavyweight champion of the world . . ."

The crowd roared as Boyd came into view. These were his people, whoever his people were.

I took off my shoes and got on the scale; 219 pounds.

Boyd stripped down to his briefs to show off his physique. God, he looked strong. The bar balanced at 228 pounds; seven more than he'd ever weighed for a fight.

Maybe that said something about the way he'd trained. If he wasn't in perfect shape, that was good. Every edge helps.

I put my shoes back on. Then I heard Boyd's voice. "White boy!"

To look or not. That was the question.

"White boy! I'm talking to you."

Probably, I should look him right in the eyes so he didn't think I was intimidated.

I turned to face him.

Boyd had pulled down his underpants and was holding his cock.

"When you're in the hospital, I'm shoving this up your girlfriend's ass."

I didn't lose it. I didn't go crazy. What happened next was cold fury.

I spat in his face.

At least, that's what I tried to do. I was aiming for his face, but he was a full body length away and the saliva fell short.

Perfectly short. A big gob landed right on his cock.

A look of total shock crossed Boyd's face.

"Good shot," Turner said. "Let's get out of here."

"Wait a minute," Vernon Jack ordered. "We got to have the staredown."

Now Boyd was screaming. "You'll die for that. I'll smash your fucking nose into your brain."

"You got your television soundbite," Turner told Jack. "Ain't nothing a staredown can do that's better than that."

The following day, Friday, passed more quickly than I would have thought. Las Vegas was buzzing and the MGM Grand was filled to capacity. Carver Boyd had brought in the high-rollers, but I was largely isolated from the buzz.

Late in the morning, I went to the HBO fighter meeting, which was the last of the contractual obligations I had to fulfill before the fight. The fighter meeting is where HBO's announcing team sits down separately with each fighter to gather information for use during the telecast. Larry Merchant asked the first question.

"Are you at all worried that yesterday's spitting incident will make Carver Boyd even more brutal than might otherwise be the case?"

"Like, if I hadn't spit on his cock, he'd be nice to me?"

Merchant shrugged.

"Look," I said. "Boyd goes into the ring to hurt people. You know what I mean by that. He has an attitude. It's part of what fuels him and makes him great. But Boyd won't be the only one in the ring with an attitude on Saturday night."

Merchant smiled and I knew what he was thinking. He didn't give me a chance.

"Are you scared?" Jim Lampley asked.

"Not yet."

"Could you elaborate on that?"

"I'm always scared on the night of a fight. I was scared before I fought a guy named Lester Bailey, and his record was one and five."

The subject turned to Dexter Morgan, who'd been chosen by the Nevada State Athletic Commission to referee the fight. Morgan was a former fighter, a heavyweight with a reputation for being a straight-shooter who split things down the middle.

"We'll get a fair shake from the referee," Turner said. "The judges, I'm not so sure about. But there's nothing we can do about it except fight our fight."

At the end of the meeting, Merchant wished me good luck. He said it like he meant it. He also said it like he thought I'd need it.

On our way out of the room, I gave the HBO production coordinator my ringwalk music. That's what they play over the loudspeakers as a fighter goes to the ring. It was the song that had been playing the night that Melissa and I first made love. Robby had been nonplussed when I chose it.

"Can't you choose something that will fire you up?" he'd asked. "The theme from *Rocky* or something inspirational like that? Who does their ring walk to a love song?'

But I know where my head is at. And the rock beat gave it a nice rhythm.

After the HBO fighter meeting, Turner, Robby,

and I drove to a gym in downtown Las Vegas that had been set aside for my use. I went through a light workout; then spent the rest of the afternoon in my hotel suite with Melissa while the other members of the team came and went.

A television was playing in the background. ESPN, CNN, and just about everyone else was showing a sanitized version of my spitting on Carver Boyd's cock with a blue dot superimposed over his not-so-private parts. An X-rated copy had made its way onto the Internet.

"I can't speak for how they do things in Boyd's neighborhood," Turner noted. "But where I come from, if someone spits on your cock, you don't talk about what you might do to them. You settle things then and there."

Melissa and I ordered room service for dinner. I watched half a movie; then turned it off. Turner returned to chat. "Get some sleep if you can," he said.

At eleven o'clock, Melissa and I turned in for the night.

"How are you holding up?" I asked.

"If you can make it through the night, I can too," she said.

Things were running wild through my mind. I couldn't shake the idea that, if Carver Boyd brought his A-game and I brought my A-game, he was winning the fight.

"There's gonna be a sign in flashing lights that says *your brain bleeds tonight.*"

Hours after midnight, I fell asleep.

Part Five

I woke up on Saturday morning a little before seven o'clock. Melissa was holding me. She hadn't slept all night.

Turner came to the suite, and I ordered breakfast for three from room service. The fight was scheduled to start at 8:15pm. There were twelve hours ahead of us.

"I want to ask you something," Turner said. "Do you want to get the fight started or do you want to get it over with?"

"I want to get it started."

"Good. That's the way it should be."

Time moved slowly.

Early in the afternoon, Jerry Izenberg came by to chat. He'd retired from the *Newark Star-Ledger* several years earlier, but still wrote occasionally. I was one of his kids and a product of Newark. He had to write about the fight.

"I like what happened at the weigh-in," Turner told him. "Not so much for us as for what it did to the other guy's head. If we can get our jab working tonight and crack Boyd with a few righthands, it will give him something to think about."

After an hour, Jerry left. Turner walked him to the door. They didn't know I was listening, but I heard everything.

"Don't let him get hurt," Jerry said.

"Don't worry. I've got his back. You know; if we make it through the early rounds, it could be an interesting night."

"From your lips to God's ear."

I took a nap. Late in the afternoon, Craig came by to wish me luck.

"Thanks for everything you've done for me," I said.

"No; thank you, man. This has been the ride of my life."

At 5:30, Turner and Robby knocked on my door, carrying duffel bags with our equipment.

"We've come a long way since that day you walked into the gym for the first time," Turner told me. "Back then, you were a scared angry kid. Now you're a man. I see bits and pieces of some great fighters in you. I want you to show it tonight."

I kissed Melissa goodbye.

"See you after the fight," I said.

There was fear in her eyes, and a tremor swept through me. Carver Boyd. Suddenly, I felt weak.

"Whatever happens," I told her, "as long as I'm with you afterward, my life is good."

I'd been putting off dealing with the fear. Now was the time to confront it.

Turner, Robby, and I arrived at dressing room number 4 in the MGM Grand Garden Arena at six o'clock. Turner opened his bag and took out the tools of his trade. Robby did the same, removing everything he might need to deal with cuts and swelling on my face in the battle ahead. I sat on a folding metal chair and stretched out my legs on the floor in front of me.

87

I took off my street clothes. Over the next hour, I put on my ring shoes, protective cup and cobalt-blue trunks.

There was quiet conversation. Two Nevada State Athletic Commission inspectors were the only other people there.

I did some stretching exercises.

Turner taped my hands.

Referee Dexter Morgan came in to give us our pre-fight instructions. "This fight is for the heavyweight championship of the world," he began. "You know the rules, and I want you to follow them. The fans don't come to see the referee." When he finished, he asked if there were any questions.

"Yes, sir," Turner said. "Boyd likes to follow through with his elbow and crack his opponent on the jaw with it. And he likes to come up hard under his opponent's chin and smash him on the jaw with the top of his head. Can we count on you to warn him about those things before the fight and take points away the first time he does it?"

"I'll see that the rules are enforced," Morgan promised.

I did some more stretching exercises and shadow-boxed for a few minutes.

Fighters tend to follow the same rituals every time in the dressing room, but they don't always feel the same. This time, everything felt good.

Turner gloved me up and I hit the pads with Robby. He advanced and I moved laterally, picking spots to stand my ground. But it was easier to stand my ground against Robby than it would be against Carver Boyd.

Turner helped me into my robe.

In fifteen minutes, I'd be in the ring. Turner put his hands on my shoulders.

"Listen to me, son. I've never steered you wrong. In eleven years, I've never lied to you. You're good enough to beat this man. You can win this fight. But you're going to have to go places inside yourself that you've never been to before."

I waited and he went on.

"Boyd will come out hard at the opening bell and try to destroy you. He's used to getting his way. The most important thing is, you can't be intimidated. There will be a storm early, and you've got to get through it. But it's not just about surviving the early part of the fight. At the end of six rounds, I want to see some damage on Boyd's face. I don't want you to get

89

into a punching competition. But unless you haul off and crack this motherfucker in the mouth with a righthand from time to time, it's going to be a problem. Get it in his head that he's in a fight."

"Boyd expects you to use every inch of the ring. Don't. You don't go anywhere near the corners or ropes. Don't let him back you into a corner. If there's a time when you can't move laterally to stay out of a corner, pick a spot, stand your ground, get off first, and knock him back. If he hits you, he hits you. If you're in a corner, you're gonna get hit anyway, so you might as well fight it out before you get there. If you feel your back against the ropes, you're in the wrong place. I want you to fight like there's barbed wire on the ropes. If you're on the ropes, throw something, tie him up, turn him and spin out. Do whatever you have to do, but get off the ropes in a hurry."

"Boyd is tough. But like a lot of bullies, he's not so tough when he gets hit. When he gets hit, he stops, resets, and starts over. Every time Boyd sets his feet, you hit him with something; even if it's just a jab to the body. Then you take a half step to the left or right, and he has to reset. When he rolls to his left, he's coming with the hook. When he rolls to his right, it's the overhand right. Either way, you step inside it or get off first."

"You can't trade with him on the inside. He's dangerous on the inside with those short fast compact punches. If he gets inside, you get closer, smother him, and tie him up. Even Boyd needs room to punch. When he dips low on the inside, push his head down. It will stop him from punching; it will put strain on his neck; and it will keep him from coming up and butting you in the jaw with the top of his head. If the referee tells you to stop pushing his head down, say 'yes, sir' and keep doing it until he threatens to take a point away. In a clinch, when the referee says break, don't just break. Be physical; push him back. And before you break, turn him so your back is facing the center of the ring, not the ropes. And another thing; you're taller than he is. If it gets rough on the inside, stuff your shoulder into his nose."

"You can't take a second off. Hold your right hand high to your temple when he's close because he has a monster left hook. At the start of each round, don't be slow getting off your stool. Be in the center of the ring waiting for him, so it gets in his head that you're there to fight."

Turner paused for a moment to let it all sink in. Then he caressed my cheek.

"There's going to be times tonight when you have to outfight him. I don't mean standing there going toe-to-toe. I mean sucking it up and fighting through pain and going places where you'd rather not have to go. I want you to test Carver Boyd's heart. Once you get past all the hate and anger that fuel him, I got a feeling he's not that strong at his core. And that woman of yours gives you a belief in yourself. I saw it in the gym from the moment she came into your life. So let's see what's stronger tonight; hate or love."

I walked to the ring with my ringwalk music playing over the loudspeaker system. A commission inspector parted the ropes and I stepped between them onto the canvas. A huge gob of blood and snot, the residue of an earlier fight, hung from the top strand near my corner. I circled the enclosure, testing the canvas for dead spots.

Then I heard a guttural roar; the kind of sound that only 16,000 people in a jam-packed arena can make. Carver Boyd's image appeared on a giant screen overhead. The ugly strains of gangsta rap rocketed through the air like machine-gun fire. Carver Boyd came into view.

He was wearing black trunks with a white cutout towel over his head. His body glistened with Vaseline and sweat. He looked indestructible and as foreboding as any man ever.

Boyd stepped onto the killing field. The ring announcer introduced us.

"Wearing blue trunks; from Fort Lee, New Jersey; with a record of thirty-one wins in thirty-one fights, fifteen of those wins coming by way of knockout; the challenger . . ."

My name was greeted with cheers and applause.

"And from Beaumont, Texas; with forty-four victories and forty-three big knockouts in forty-four fights; the undisputed heavyweight champion of the world . . ."

The roar of the crowd drowned out Boyd's name.

Dexter Morgan called us to the center of the ring for his final instructions.

There was one last staredown.

"I'm gonna fuck you up, white boy."

"Shut up, Carver," Morgan said.

We returned to our corners.

"My heart's in your gloves," Turner told me. "Kick his ass."

The bell rang and Carver Boyd came toward me. I met him with a jab. He fired a righthand that missed, and I moved laterally. He kept coming forward, bobbing, weaving, throwing punches. He didn't land anything solid, but the glancing blows told me that he hit as hard as people said he did. I kept moving, jabbing, doing what I had to do. He got inside and I tied him up. In the clinch, I could feel that he was physically stronger than I was. I was using more energy staying out of trouble than he was using to attack.

After the round, Turner took out my mouthpiece and Robby rinsed it. "Take a deep breath," Turner told me. "That's one round down. Stay on your toes. Keep moving. Keep throwing your jab. So far, so good."

Round two started with more of the same, but it was getting harder to keep Boyd off. No matter how I moved, he closed the distance between us. My jab wasn't keeping him away. I fired a righthand and missed. Even the punches I blocked with my arms hurt. I'd known he was fast, but his hands were faster than I'd thought. I landed another jab. Boyd came back with a hook up top, and suddenly I was in trouble. The right side of my face went numb. I staggered back into the ropes, and he was all over me. I was aware of everything, but it seemed to be happening without me. I felt my back against the ropes. Boyd fired two more punches in rapid succession; a right and a left with knockout written all over them. I slipped the first, dipped under the second, and threw a desperation righthand that landed. He paused for a fraction of a second to reset, and I escaped to my right behind a jab.

"Keep your fucking right hand glued to your head when you're not throwing it," Turner shouted at me between rounds. "And move your head after you punch; because if you miss, he'll be punching back." His decibel level lowered a bit. "That righthand you caught him with was good. It got you out of trouble and gave him something to think about. But don't trade with him unless you have to. The jab is the key. And stay off the ropes."

Round three. Boyd resumed his attack with blood trickling from his mouth. My desperation righthand had split his lip. But reality was settling in. I've heard it said that fighters are so psyched during a fight that we don't feel pain. I was feeling pain. Boyd's punches hurt. I was doing everything right; moving laterally, firing jabs into his collarbone and face. Whatever I did, he had an answer for it. Nothing stopped him. He was like the tide rolling in, a force of nature moving inexorably forward.

After the round, Turner put a bottle of water to my lips and I took a sip. "Don't stand in close with him. When he gets in close, tie him up or put your left foot between his legs, step into him, and push him back with your forearm."

It wasn't working. In round four, I did what I could, but it was getting harder and harder to keep Boyd off. I stopped him momentarily with a righthand lead and double-jab. He came back with a hook that fell short. *Whack!* An elbow followed and caught me on the cheekbone just below my right eye. There was no time to complain. A killer right came after it. I slipped my head to the side to avoid the blow, wedged his left arm under my right, and pushed my shoulder against his jaw to tie him up. Turner's voice sounded above the crowd. "Elbow! Elbow! Damn it, ref."

Robby applied an Enswell to my cheekbone

between rounds. If the tissue swelled up, it would impair the vision out of my right eye. "This is where you dig deep," Turner told me.

Round five. I was fighting as well as I could, but it wasn't enough. I was learning why Carver Boyd was the best fighter in the world. His punches were taking a toll. Punch after punch. Too many of them were landing. I was getting beaten up. A hook to the body sent an excruciating bolt of pain through me; pain like I'd never felt before; pain that I'll remember till the day I die. I went down. The roar of the crowd was pounding in my brain. Dexter Morgan stood over me, counting and flashing fingers in my face.

"Three . . . Four . . ."

I got up at eight.

"Do you want to continue?"

"Yes, sir."

Morgan wiped my gloves against his shirt and gestured for Boyd to come forward. He was on top of me in an instant. I stepped inside another hook that would have taken my head off if it had landed. I tied him up, held on for my life, and he shook me like a rag doll.

"Break!" Morgan ordered.

I kept holding, and the referee moved in to physically separate us. Boyd relaxed for an instant in anticipation of the break. He was eager to get on with the business of hurting. I shifted my weight, leveraged him over my leg, and threw him to the canvas.

"No, no, no," Morgan shouted. "You can't do that."

"Can I say something, sir."

"What is it?" the referee demanded.

"He tried to break my arm off at the elbow."

Not true. But to emphasize the point, I raised my left arm and touched my right glove to my elbow. Morgan gave me a skeptical look. Then he motioned for Boyd and me to come toward him and grabbed us each by the forearm.

"I want no rough stuff from either of you. Do you hear me? Obey the rules."

The action resumed. I'd gotten an extra fifteen seconds to recover. Now we're even, Carver. I owed you one for whacking me in the face with your elbow.

Between rounds, the doctor assigned to my corner stood on the ring apron and listened as Turner talked to me. "You stayed in the same spot without throwing. That's why you got hit. Keep him turning and moving, so he can't set his feet. Lateral movement all the time. And keep popping that jab."

Round six. Boyd came out for the kill, firing punches hard and fast. I was circling clockwise, counterclockwise, jabbing, doing everything I could to slow his pursuit. A look of frustration, crossed his face. "Come on and fight, pussy," he sneered. I kept moving. The assault continued at a slightly slower pace. Near the end of the round, he took a breather for a moment when he was in range and I cracked him with my best punch of the fight, a solid righthand that stopped him in his tracks. I can hurt you, Carver. Maybe not all at once with one punch like you do it. But I can hurt you.

"That was a good righthand," Turner told me between rounds. "He tasted your power just then, and he didn't like it. Now listen to me. The fight is half over and you're doing what you have to do. You've weathered the storm. He's starting to lose his edge. The second half of the fight is yours. Keep fighting smart. You have six more rounds to do your job."

Round seven. I was still landing my jab. The skin around Boyd's left eye was puffing up and he was a bit easier to hit. I'm not getting faster, so he must be slowing down. I jabbed again, then doubled up, setting down hard on the second jab. That felt real good. I didn't wait for a receipt. Kept moving. Then I saw blood. Look at that! I just broke Carver Boyd's nose. He worked his way inside, and I tied him up. Instead of struggling to free himself, he locked onto my arms and lifted his body up, using the top of his head as a battering ram against my chin.

It felt like my teeth were going through my mouthpiece.

"Time!" the referee said. "Intentional head-butt. One point deduction."

"He banged into my head," Boyd protested.

"Don't give me that crap," Morgan chastized. "I was fighting before you were born. I saw what you did."

In the corner after the round, Robby put Vaseline on my face. "That was a two-point round for you," Turner told me. "He's still dangerous, but you're starting to break him down. Keep your right hand high and keep throwing."

Round eight. My jab was landing consistently, raising the swelling around Boyd's left eye. There was a constant flow of blood from his nose and a trickle from his lower lip. He landed an overhand right that hurt, but not as much as the blows before. I took it and fired back with a righthand. I belonged in the ring with Carver Boyd, and both of us knew it.

"There you go," Turner said after the round. "Boyd is tough, but he's not so tough once he gets hit. Don't get careless. Keep doing your thing. He's only programmed to fight one way. He has no Plan B."

Round nine. Boyd was tired and his upper-body movement had diminished, making him an easier target. His left eye was closing. I can't see my own face, but his doesn't look so good. I started mixing more righthands in with my jab. I've taken your best shots, Carver; and I'm still here. You're good, Carver; but I can beat you.

Turner sat me down on the stool when the next one-minute rest period came. "This fight is close," he said. "And right now, you're in better shape than he is. You've won the last three rounds. The next three rounds are for the heavyweight championship of the world."

Round ten. I was pounding my jab into Boyd's face and advancing more forcefully than I'd been able to do before. Blood from his nose was mingling with blood from his lower lip. He wasn't bobbing and weaving much any more. You talk a good fight, Carver. Now that the going is tough, let's see you back it up. I was taking more chances, firing lead righthands and committing more on my jab. I never listen to the crowd. Early on, I'd been vaguely aware that they were cheering for Boyd. Now, in the back of my mind, I heard them chanting my name. The bell rang. Going back to my corner, I had the feeling that Boyd was growing smaller.

Robby pressed the Enswell against the skin beneath my eye as he'd done after every round. Turner gave me a sip of water. "It's time," he said. "Beat this motherfucker up."

Round eleven. The all-out aggression that had given Boyd the lead was gone. The combinations were gone. Now he was loading up and throwing one punch at a time, trying to keep my jab out of his face and hoping to catch me in a mistake. He was telegraphing his punches. I could see them coming. My jab was stopping him in his tracks, backing him up. Does that hurt, Carver? How about that one? Bobbing and weaving isn't so easy when the other guy keeps punching you in the face.

Then it happened. Boyd set his feet to punch. His eyes said jab; his hands said jab. The muscles on his chest said overhand right. I saw the trap. And I figured I could beat it. You throw your best righthand, Carver; I'll throw mine; and we'll see who lands first.

One moment of violence can change everything.

I pulled the trigger a split second before he did. That was the difference. And I knew what was coming. He didn't.

A lot of punches land solid in a fight. But the leverage isn't quite right or the punch is a fraction of an inch off target. This one was perfect. Perfect leverage; perfect timing; perfect placement. My knuckles landed flush against Boyd's jaw. A jolt of electricity ran up my arm all the way to my shoulder. The blow carried every ounce of anger, pain, loss, and love that I'd accumulated in twenty-five years of living. It was the best punch I've ever thrown.

Boyd's knees buckled and he staggered back against the ropes. I moved in behind a rangefinder jab and whacked him flush on the jaw with another righthand.

His tree-trunk legs held him up. I dug a left hook into his gut and felt him sag. Another big righthand up top.

Like a prehistoric monster sinking into a swamp, Boyd started to fall. He reached reflexively for the top ring rope to hold himself up with his left hand. His head was completely exposed. I unloaded one last perfectly leveraged righthand that landed smack in the center of his face and drove him to the canvas.

There was bedlam in the arena, the loudest blast of sound I'd ever heard; a crashing booming tumultuous roar that reverberated and kept getting louder.

The referee motioned me to a neutral corner.

I couldn't hear the count.

"Four . . ."

There it was.

"Five . . ."

Pay attention. If he gets up, there's two minutes left in the round to finish him off.

"Six . . ."

He's on his hands and knees.

"Seven . . ."

Either way, Carver. If you get up, I'll knock you down again.

"Eight . . ."

I've seen that look on guys before. He's thinking about staying down.

"Nine . . ."

Part Six

In the dressing room after the fight, it was just the core group. Turner, Robby, Craig, Melissa, myself; and the same inspectors from the state athletic commission who'd been there before.

A commission doctor came into the room to make sure I was all right. I was holding an icepack against my right eye to reduce the swelling and feeling every punch I'd taken during the fight.

"I'm okay," I assured the doctor. "A little beat up, but I feel good."

Melissa had been crying on and off.

"I can't believe it," she said.

"Believe it," Turner told her.

His next words were spoken with a smile as wide as the sky.

"Your man is the new heavyweight champion of the world."

Craig looked up from the bench, where he'd been going over the judges' scorecards.

"One judge gave you the first round," he said. "The other two gave it to Boyd. Each judge gave Boyd rounds two through six. You ran the table from seven on. He got an extra point for the knockdown in round five, and the referee took a point away from him for the head-butt in round seven."

So we'd gotten honest scoring after all. Going into round eleven, I'd been two points down on two judges' scorecards and even on the third. If Boyd had gotten up from the knockdown and survived till the bell, everything would have been up for grabs in the final round.

As it was, he stayed down.

Could he have gotten up? I don't know. I'd like to think that, under the same circumstances, I'd have made it to my feet.

A third inspector entered the dressing room with a smile on his face and an envelope in his hand.

"Here you are, champ. Sign for this and it's all yours."

I signed and he handed me a check for $1,455,000. One-point-five million dollars minus the three percent sanctioning fee.

"And that's just the start," Craig said. "For your next fight, I figure you'll be guaranteed fifteen million plus an upside. That's if you fight a bum. A rematch with Boyd would put thirty million dollars in your pocket."

"I'm not greedy," I told him. "Fifteen million for a bum is fine with me."

I handed the check to Melissa.

"Don't lose this."

"And five million dollars more in endorsement income," Craig added. "You don't know it; but about an hour ago, you became a national hero."

There was a knock on the door, and one of Vernon Jack's publicity men entered. "Excuse me, champ. They're waiting for you at the post-fight press conference."

"With egg on their face," Craig noted. "A hundred writers; and I'm guessing that every one of them picked Carver Boyd to win by knockout."

"The writers are writing history tonight," Turner said.

I stood up and started toward the shower; then

111

stopped, walked over to Melissa, and put my arms around her. She wasn't someone who'd come into my life for the big money and bright lights like a lot of people would be trying to do in the months ahead. She'd been with me since I was a club fighter in Newark. I've been fortunate in that, despite my hard beginnings, a lot of good people have cared about me over the years. Melissa loved me.

We embraced, neither one of us wanting to let go. Finally . . .

"I'm getting you all bloody and greasy," I said.

"I don't care."

"Neither do I."

Boxing and Melissa. Two love stories.